T0209766

X.mouse DOWNUNDER

MEGAN CALDWELL

Balboa Press books may be ordered through booksellers or by contacting:

Balboa Press
A Division of Hay House
1663 Liberty Drive
Bloomington, IN 47403
www.balboapress.com.au
1 (877) 407-4847

ISBN: 978-1-5043-1596-8 (sc)
978-1-5043-1595-1 (e)

Print information available on the last page.

Balboa Press rev. date: 11/26/2018

BALBOA
PRESS
A DIVISION OF HAY HOUSE

To Mindy Christie, Charli Morrow

and all the children around the world

who need love, belief and encouragement.

Special thanks to Sherryn Danaher, Kim Trezise,

Anne Reid and Jude Obieche for help along the way.

Should you ever travel to the

South Pole, where it is extremely c-o-o-old,

you will almost certainly meet the Xmouse Family.

Before Xmas, the Xmouse family are going mad,

making presents for the good children

in the Southern part of the world.

The Grandpa is a lovely old mouse, who wears a warm

yellow scarf. He supervises making
sure the presents are made

well and wrapped with love and pretty paper.

Mary Xmouse is a happy house mouse who has over

nine hundred and ninety of her own children. She spends
her time cooking for her family, making sure her children
are clean and that their nails are always cut short.

Her husband is **Count Xmouse**.

He spends his time counting the holes in his enorMOUSE

collection of Swiss cheese.

He often forgets how much he has counted

because there is soooo much cheese.

Can you help him?

Santa Claws is a big grey cat with long
claws from the South Pole.

He supervises the Xmouses. He makes sure they do

everything right and no time is wasted.

His sister **Sandra Claws** lives in the

North Pole. She has the same role as Santa Claws,

but her work is in the Northern countries of the world.

The Xmousettes, the teenage Xmouses,

set off to deliver presents.

What do you think the fish is thinking as the Xmousettes

go under water with all the presents?

They are taking presents in a very special and unusual way, not in the sky as you may have thought, but under the ocean where nobody could ever spy on them.

The trains are powered by sea horses to produce bubbles because you can't use steam under the ocean.

On their way, they saw an octopus playing a banjo

shark accompanied by some blue bottles.

It was a rare and interesting sight.

Finally, they arrive in Melbourne.

Waiting for them was a red shiny Holden Ute

and some rather strange **Australian Xmousettes**.

After scrambling up, they nibbled the chocolate

which was kindly left for them.

"Mmmm...it tastes good."

Voices of children approaching, so they ran and hid.

"I wonder whether Santa has been yet?"

"Could there be a bike or a doll's house?"

The children sounded happy to see the toys the

Xmousettes had brought.

At the same time, they were disappointed

because all the things they had wished for, weren't there.

There were little bite marks in the chocolate and

some of the juice they left.

Then their little white dog, Lilly, came to see them.

She had a note tucked into her collar. The

children freed the note and read it.

It was a note from the Xmousettes.

"Who?" The children asked each other.

Dear Sarah and Charli,
We are the Xmouxettes, We know
you don't have many presents under
the tree this year. Many children
have never had any presents.
This year we thought it was fair
for all the children around the
world to have at least one
present. This way every one gets at
least a gift and love from the
xmouses and Santa claws.

Tin Kertoy tonk
The xmousettes.

"Perhaps there is something we can do next year... maybe we can come up with some ideas of toys for the Xmouses to make!"

The children said excitedly.

The children ran happily outside with Lilly and their news toys.

THE END

Ideas for teaching

Ask students if they can think of any simple presents that all children would enjoy. An attempt could then be made to practice the ideas.

Maybe other cultures could be talked about.

Practise colour naming and counting throughout the book

#The Xmouses were so called because they were born angry and therefore very cross.

ABOUT THE AUTHOR

This is Megan's first book. She writes with a vivid imagination inspired by her mother's inventive play during her childhood. She has fond memories of dolls' houses made from shoe boxes, and foot prints from the Easter Kangaroo leading the way to her Easter Eggs. Her Grandma Dottie and Grandpa Jim enthralled her and her sister with magical stories of pixies that were full of mischief and fun. Megan has taken her sense of childhood wonder and created Xmouse Downunder, a beautiful work of humour and art, to continue the family tradition.

Megan was taught how to paint as a child by her Grandma Gwen. When she was twenty years of age, she was involved in a serious car accident and sustained a life changing Severe Traumatic Brain Injury. She later met her husband Wayne and they have a teenage son Jeromi. She returned to painting about six years after the accident and strongly connects with this part of her identity. She now has an art studio on her property where she continues to create works and is excited to add the role of author to her artistic resume.

Printed in the United States
By Bookmasters